Rock City

Anne Eton

This paperback is also available as an ebook at most online ebook retailers.

Copyright 2013 Beginnings Press

ISBN-13: 978-1-62602-036-8

ISBN-10: 1626020361

Julie Espinoza fought her way through the throng of cheering, crazed spring breakers. *There's thousands of them,* she thought. Despite the jostling, however, a big smile illuminated her face. This was one of the happiest days of her life.

The thump of "Girls Just Wanna Have Fun" reverberated over the crowd as Cyndi Lauper sang her guts out on the big stage. And she, Julie, just happened to have dressed exactly like Cyndi that day—down to the hoop earrings and warrior makeup and stretched-neck sweater pulled over the shoulder! What were the odds!

True, Julie did not LOOK like Cyndi Lauper. Julie was frankly hotter, even if she said so herself. But she didn't have to—in slam books all through high school, and now in the informal polls at Daytona Beach Community College, she was consistently ranked Sexiest Girl...if one did not count that total bitch, LeeAnn Travis, who about half the time bumped Julie down to number two in the rankings. *One of these days I'm gonna knock the peroxide out of her hair,* Julie thought to herself. Her mood darkened.

LeeAnn.

Like streptococcus, LeeAnn Travis had plagued Julie all of Julie's life. LeeAnn's blonde hair, big even by 80's MTV standards; her gigantic boobs; her wicked smile; those ridiculously revealing clothes…well, she was every other girl's nightmare, wasn't she? Especially for Julie, who was seriously considering going out to Hollywood next year and trying her luck in the movie business. If LeeAnn ever heard about it, LeeAnn would decide to come out also. Even though LeeAnn would never get any part, unless maybe as Dolly Parton's trashy kid sister.

Julie closed her eyes. She breathed. *Don't think about LeeAnn. You are the hottest girl in Daytona. Hell, in Florida! So what if she's blond and looks like a blow-up doll? YOU are a smoking, sultry, half-Latina brunette who made the captain of the All-State football team kneel before you. In front of his friends. Remember that? Oye Como Va! So walk tall, girl. You are about to have an excellent three days.*

Six months ago, Julie had spotted a flyer on the main bulletin board in her community college's student union. A gigantic rock festival was coming to Daytona Beach that spring. Based on the Woodstock festival, the Daytona venue would have 5 stages, famous bands, and would draw tens of thousands of spring break kids. The flyer said that a few backstage volunteers were needed. Applicants should send a resume and a photo. Julie had sent a sultry MTV-vixen-ish picture she'd taken for her modeling portfolio. She had received the call two weeks before the concert: she, Julie Espinoza, would be an Official Backstage Bottled Water Attendant! True, there was no money, but think of the prestige. And the opportunity to meet rock stars. *Will Mötley Crüe be there?* Julie shivered.

The backstage entrance loomed ahead of her. Julie grinned and flashed a pass on a lanyard around her neck. She strode through three levels of security before she was finally inside.

In no time she met the Backstage Coordinator, Marv. He looked exactly like the dad in *Eight Is Enough,* only with less hair. Marv was wearing a brown ruffled shirt and green leather pants. "Nice to meet you," he said. Julie offered her hand to shake. He turned away.

Julie followed Marv through a maze of hallways. Big long-haired men hurried in all directions with guitars, black rolling cargo boxes, cheetah-print clothes in clear plastic bags on hangers, and all manner of drum kits.

"You ever work a rock concert before?" Marv yelled back at Julie as they weaved their way through the chaos.

"No, sir," Julie said. She tried not to hop up

and down with excitement; the beginning strains of David Bowie's "Let's Dance" filtered in from a stage somewhere on the massive festival grounds. *This is the greatest rock concert in the history of the world,* Julie thought to herself. *For three days, Daytona Beach is Rock City!*

"Well, listen," Marv shouted back again. "This is the primary backstage area. All the dressing rooms are here, and the VIP lounge. We are adjacent to Stage One, the big one." A gigantic roadie accidentally thumped Marv's shoulder in passing; Marv cursed at him but didn't break stride.

"Anyway," Marv continued, "you have three simple rules. A: give out water bottles from the water stand. B: when you are out of water, replenish from the supply room. C: do not under any circumstances talk to rock stars unless they talk to you first. Think you can remember that?"

Julie nodded. "Yes sir."

"Get it straight. You got this volunteer job because, obviously, you are super hot. But there are a million hot girls out there—" he pointed to the walls where the crowd's roar came through "—who would kill to be where you are now. You don't obey the rules, you're gone."

Where did this guy come from? Julie wondered. She rolled her eyes behind his back. *I am working three long days for free.* But she replied, in her sweetest tone, "I understand."

"Bitchin'." Marv turned a corner. They entered

an area that looked like a covered loading dock. Touching the dock was a scaffold. From it hung a fifty-foot-high black curtain that extended two hundred feet long. Julie had arrived directly behind Stage One. Cyndi Lauper's road crew dashed back and forth like ants through a flap in the curtain, removing amplifiers and other gear from the stage, clearing the space for the next act.

Marv stopped abruptly. He turned to a small plywood stand upon whose front the word "water" had been magic-markered in Olde English letters by some artistic soul. "Brunette, meet blonde," Marv said. He began to speak again but then he paused, puzzled.

Julie was staring. Her jaw had dropped.

LeeAnn, behind the plywood water stand, stared back.

The girls stood frozen.

"What, you know each other?" Marv said.

"Oh my God." Julie turned to Marv. "Please tell me I am not working with her."

He shrugged. "Like I said: you got this job because your picture was super hot. Probably like hers."

Say WHAT? Julie thought, her jaw dropping even lower.

Marv frowned. Looking from Julie to LeeAnn, he intoned: "You guys got a problem working together? If you do, tell me now. I'll take your passes and I'll go pull some chicks out of the crowd here. Somehow, I don't think it will be a hard sell."

"No, of course not sir," LeeAnn said quickly. She offered her sexiest smile. Marv could not help smiling back. She was good.

"No problem at all," Julie added. She smiled and shifted her hips, adopting a sultry pose, all the while thinking: *no way I am going to quit and let this bitch have it all to herself.*

"Good," Marv said. He told them where more water was: next to the VIP lounge, down the hall to the left. "Here," he said to Julie as he handed her the stockroom key. "Bathrooms are in the other direction. If people ask you any other questions, direct them to me. I'll be back. What are you waiting for?"

Julie blinked. He was talking to her. "What?"

"What are you waiting for?" Marv repeated. He pointed. "Get behind the counter with her!"

Julie hurried, stepping around Marv and sliding behind the little water stand next to her most hated enemy. Her hip accidentally brushed LeeAnn's. Julie tried not to throw up.

"Comfy?" Marv smiled indulgently. "I must say, the organizers chose well. You two look like you stepped out of an MTV video or something. Blonde and brunette, who could ask for anything more? Don't let it get to your head though, I have plenty to choose from out there. Start handing out water. I'll see you later."

Marv dashed off.

Julie stood stock-still. She did not look at

LeeAnn. *How the hell did this happen,* Julie asked herself. She guessed that LeeAnn must have seen the same flyer in the student union. They attended the same community college, after all. Julie hadn't even considered the possibility that LeeAnn would apply. *Ugh.*

Julie had known that she should have ripped down that flyer for herself the moment she saw it. But some stupid sense of fairness had prevented her. *Thanks, mom and dad, for the moral instruction that is now ruining my life.*

A roadie wandered by, asking for water. Julie offered him a bottle, but LeeAnn beat her to it. Of course she did. Whatever Julie wanted to do, LeeAnn just had to do better, didn't she?

Julie studied her adversary out of the corner of her eye. Clearly, LeeAnn was in a Samantha Fox phase. Her blonde hair rose above her head in a big fireworks bouffant. Eyeliner and mascara vied for supremacy on her face. But her tight red jumpsuit, cut RIDICULOUSLY low, was the real showstopper. She must have had it custom-made. It fit her body like a glove, even with the oversized shoulder pads. The blonde's hourglass figure was drawing stares from all and sundry as they hurried by on their backstage missions.

Julie felt like a vise was crushing her skull so that her head would explode, like in that new movie *Scanners.* Finally, she couldn't take it anymore.

"Balloons or zombies?" Julie asked the empty

air in front of her. She looked down and picked at a fingernail.

LeeAnn turned. "I'm sorry. Were you talking to me?" She stretched her red-gloss lips wide in a fake smile.

Julie studied her fingernail. "I was just wondering…are you going for balloons, or zombies?"

LeeAnn began to change colors. *Good,* Julie thought. Julie knew that LeeAnn's brain was her weak spot. It had always been, since fourth grade, way before her ridiculous assets had appeared. LeeAnn was terribly sensitive about looking stupid.

"Have you been spending too much time in the sun?" the blonde asked. She made a poor-you face. "That black hair of yours must boil your head something awful."

Oh, you bitch, Julie thought. Just as Julie knew LeeAnn's weakest spot, LeeAnn knew Julie's. Julie Espinoza had always wanted blonde hair. She had tried a do-it-yourself dye job once, in junior high. The result? Disaster. LeeAnn had never let Julie or anybody else forget it.

Time for the kill. Julie turned to LeeAnn, smiling sweetly. "I'm sorry, you probably didn't understand." Julie laughed a high little trill. "You see, that jumpsuit of yours? Obviously you're trying to be either Michael Jackson in 'Thriller,' or the '99 Balloons' girl. So, I'm just wondering…is it balloons? Or zombies?"

LeeAnn's face transformed into a hideous mask of mottled rage. "You knew I was coming here," she hissed. "You found out. And you just had to ruin it."

Julie arched her back, a snarling cat. "Barf me out! As if anything you do would ever pass my mind. Because I have a mind."

"Really?" LeeAnn smiled again. "If it passed your mind, then how did you think about it?"

Julie felt confusion and anger at once. True, the "pass my mind" thing hadn't come out right. But her blood was up, okay? Of course, LeeAnn wouldn't give any quarter. Oooohhhh. LEEANN. How the hell! Her and LeeAnn, stuck together for three days? They hadn't even been here a minute and already a double homicide was only seconds away.

"S'cuse me?"

They turned to a customer. A slightly frightened-looking fellow with an odd accent.

"Yes?" Julie said. She touched her hair with a shaky hand.

"May I have some water, please?"

"Of course!" Julie handed him a bottle from under the stand before LeeAnn could beat her to it.

"Ta." He opened it. "Cheers." Tipping the bottle, he guzzled it dry without coming up for air.

"Where are you from?" LeeAnn asked, pointedly ignoring Julie.

"Ah. Scotland," the guy said. He wiped his mouth on his t-shirt sleeve. "Scotland the brave, yeah!"

LeeAnn laughed like it was the wittiest thing she'd ever heard. The guy had a stick figure, bad teeth, and an awful haircut. But Julie sensed that LeeAnn was shifting into alpha-girl mode. LeeAnn wanted the guy's attention. Well, it wasn't going to work.

"What band are you with?" Julie purred. She turned her hips a little, letting him see her profile. He appraised it. Julie was glad she'd worn a short skirt.

"Sheena Easton," the man said. "Say, here she comes now!"

The girls looked and gasped. Yes. There she was. Sheena Easton!

Sheena looked fabulous, dressed in a rainbow-band cotton sweatshirt with a stretched-out neck over one shoulder and stripey leg warmers. She approached unsteadily on clear-plastic high heels.

"Oh my God," LeeAnn gasped.

"Don't talk to the rock stars," Julie said. A tremor shook her voice.

"'Ello ladies," Sheena said in a thick Scottish brogue.

"Unless they talk to you first," LeeAnn said to Julie, shooting her a withering look.

"Ya been chattin' up me lad Craig here, hae ya?" Sheena asked.

"Uh. Yeah! Yeah, I guess so," LeeAnn said.

"Would you like some water?" Julie asked stupidly.

"Nay."

"Okay," Julie said.

"Say," Sheena remarked. "Whyn't'cha gae me lad here a snog, like?"

"I'm sorry," LeeAnn said. "I only speak English."

Julie kicked her. "She IS speaking English."

Craig the roadie laughed. "She's saying, why don't you two make out and give me a show?"

"Nay, I meant them snog YOU," Sheena said to him.

He shook his head. "I'd rather they kiss each other. Give me a nice picture to remember Rockstock by." He winked.

Sheena shrugged. "Ah well, have it your way." She turned to the girls, leaning on their counter. "Go on, then! He works hard for little money, God knows. Ya have to give him somethin'. Show him some Christian kindness."

The girls did not move.

Sheena batted her eyes. "Pleeeaaaase? Aren't you modern girls?"

Julie and LeeAnn laughed, releasing tension. Sheena had referenced her hit song.

The girls looked at each other. A long moment passed.

Finally, LeeAnn shrugged.

Julie said, "Okay."

They moved their faces toward each other,

trying to otherwise not touch. Closing their eyes at the last moment, their lips met. They held the kiss for one second before pulling apart.

"Ah, lovely, lovely," Craig said. He sighed, as if he'd just had a beer after a long day.

"Nay, that was nothin'!" Sheena said. A roar from behind the curtain made her glance. "Right. I gotta go. But you two, be ready to give us some real stuff when I come back!"

She laughed and turned to the curtain. Two assistants held it open for her. As she passed through it the crowd went berserk. Julie and LeeAnn caught a glimpse of thousands of college kids cheering and waving. Easton's band immediately launched into "Modern Girl."

Craig hurried away.

LeeAnn slowly set Craig's emptied water bottle under the counter. She did not look at Julie.

After a very long minute, Julie mumbled: "I'm going to go to the bathroom, uh, if that's okay…"

"Yeah sure," LeeAnn said, also not making eye contact.

Inside of a locked stall, Julie sat down and took a deep breath.

Kissing LeeAnn Travis? It was worse than a nightmare. If ever this got out…

Oh my gosh.

With luck, Sheena Easton would forget about a repeat make-out after her set. And Julie would just give away water with LeeAnn, and neither of them would ever talk about this again.

Julie's mind paused. Julie had kissed a few boys in her time. More than a few, honestly. But LeeAnn's lips had been softer than any lips that Julie had even thought possible. Julie wondered if all girls were like that, or if LeeAnn was simply special.

Special! Yeah, LeeAnn's special all right. As in special ed.

Julie finally shook her head. She didn't know how long she had been sitting there. She didn't have a watch. Duty called.

As Julie returned, Sheena from the stage wailed the last notes of "For Your Eyes Only," the James Bond ballad.

"Hey," Julie said as she slipped behind the water stand once more.

"Hey," LeeAnn said back.

A long pause followed.

"So, this is totally going to be a secret, right?" LeeAnn said.

"Totally."

"Good." LeeAnn exhaled. She looked directly at Julie for the first time since Sheena had left. "Like, I would catch shit from my friends forever."

"Yeah, totally, me too."

"It's not even, like, kissing a girl. I mean, a lot of girls do that."

Julie did a double-take. "They do?"

"Whatever. All I'm saying is, if my friends ever found out I kissed YOU, they would never let it die."

"Pact." Julie extended her little finger.

LeeAnn raised her hand and hooked her own pinky through Julie's. With a solemn look they simultaneously said, "Swear."

LeeAnn released her finger. She smiled.

Julie smiled also.

Sheena emerged through the curtain. She made a beeline for the water stand.

"Here we go," LeeAnn muttered.

"Drink?" Sheena asked.

Julie handed her a bottle of water.

"Ahem," Craig said. He had appeared out of nowhere.

"Oh yeah," Sheena said. She focused on Julie and LeeAnn. "G'on, now. Give us a kiss. A real one. The kind that warms you up!"

LeeAnn rolled her eyes. She turned to Julie.

"So bogus," Julie said. She nevertheless moved closer to her nemesis, so that her boobs pressed gently into the considerable swell of LeeAnn's jumpsuit.

Closing their eyes again, the girls touched lips and made out for over a minute.

Finally, LeeAnn pulled away. Wiping her lips with the back of her hand, she turned.

Sheila had been joined by a phalanx of roadies, grips, electricians, groupies, and other assorted rock people.

Sheila clapped. The others followed, cheering.

LeeAnn blushed. She made a dismissive

gesture. "We're here all week, folks," she joked.

Sheila and her crew wandered away. The rest of the crowd dispersed.

"Gotta go," Julie mumbled. She dashed off toward the bathroom again.

As she left she heard LeeAnn say, "God, take a chill pill. I'm not contaminated…"

Locking herself in a women's room stall once more, Julie sat. She closed her eyes and breathed hard.

The problem wasn't that Julie thought LeeAnn was contaminated (although that of course was certainly possible).

The problem was…

Julie couldn't even admit it. But she had to.

She took a deep breath and looked at the ceiling.

The problem was that Julie felt deeply, unprecedentedly turned on.

Halfway through the make-out, something had shifted inside of her. A sudden rich kind of FLOW had coursed through her body, turning her flesh on fire.

Now, sitting in the stall, Julie closed her eyes. *You are not turned on by LeeAnn Travis,* she told herself. *That is impossible. That cannot happen.*

But even as she thought it, she felt her heart hammering at the memory of LeeAnn's soft mouth. LeeAnn's lip gloss had tasted like strawberry.

Julie felt The Feeling. The feeling of *no no, don't*

do it. She had felt The Feeling with bad boys, musicians, older men—basically any guy whom she absolutely, positively should not date.

And she had always dated them anyway.

Because the *thump-thump-thump* of her heart had always made the excitement of The Feeling impossible to resist.

This time, however, The Feeling had cranked up to 11. Julie's heart was actually going to burst out of her ribcage. That's how it felt, anyway. Julie placed a careful hand over her chest, stunned by the crazy response LeeAnn had provoked.

Julie closed her eyes. No matter how much she told herself *NO*…

She wanted, needed, had to kiss LeeAnn again. Just the thought made her skin tingle.

* * *

"Hey," LeeAnn said as Julie returned poker-faced to the water stand. "Are you totally recovered?"

Julie blinked. "What?"

"Like, are you recovered from whatever germs you thought I gave you?" LeeAnn rolled her eyes and looked away.

"Oh. No! I mean, it's cool. I just had to, uh…make a phone call."

LeeAnn regarded Julie skeptically.

"No, really," Julie continued. "I had to call my agent and stuff. So. What's going on?"

"We're out of water," LeeAnn said.

Julie looked. The full plastic bottles under the stand counter had vanished. "Yeah. Okay, why don't we go get some more."

LeeAnn looked around. "Should one of us stay here?"

Julie stared. "If we don't have any water to give out anyway, why bother?"

Leeann thought about it. She nodded.

Yikes, Julie thought. *How can I be attracted to someone this dumb?*

As they walked to where Marv had told them the stockroom would be, Julie grew more philosophical. *You've been attracted to dummies before. Remember Chad? With the motorcycle?*

Yeah, fine. But this is LeeAnn. How the hell can you be attracted to HER?

That…is an excellent question.

"You okay?"

Julie turned, startled. "What?"

LeeAnn studied Julie as they walked down a crowded hall. "You sound like you're talking to yourself."

"Just practicing some lines. I have an audition soon. Here we are!"

Julie stopped in front of a door. On it was a taped piece of paper with a single word scribbled: "Stockroom."

She withdrew her key.

Inside the girls found what looked like thousands of pounds of bottled water, stacked to the ceiling in towers. All around was an assortment of stuff: lumber, air conditioners, small refrigerators, fans…

"Oh my gosh!" LeeAnn gasped.

Julie turned around. She saw what LeeAnn did, and gasped also.

The couch measured twelve feet wide at least. Its plush rich purple color gleamed, as if no human had ever touched it. Embossed in the middle of the backrest was a guitar with angel's wings.

"Whose do you think that is?" LeeAnn asked. She turned to Julie with wide eyes. "That little logo thing looks like maybe Aerosmith, or Led Zeppelin. You know? With the wings?"

"They're not appearing here," Julie said. She gazed unblinking at the custom-made rock couch. "If they were in the lineup, I would've remembered."

"God. Then whose is it?"

Julie shook her head. "I don't know. The stockroom here is next to the VIP lounge. Maybe the festival had it made for the lounge, and then it didn't fit?"

"What a waste!"

Julie giggled. "I would LOVE this in my living room."

"No duh. I can't fit it in my room but I would freakin' knock the wall out, or something. It's gorgeous!"

"You live with your parents?"

LeeAnn suddenly looked defensive. "Yeah, so

what?"

"So, nothing. Hey. Want to sit on it?"

LeeAnn's eyes lit up. "God, it looks brand-new. They'll know. Won't they?"

"Who cares!" Without waiting for an answer, Julie leaped. Spinning in midair, she landed butt-first on the plush purple cushions. The springs creaked.

Julie's body sank into the soft fuzzy cushions. Before she could squeal in ecstasy, she felt the couch's springs creak again, as LeeAnn flung herself upon the other end.

The girl screamed together.

"TUBULAR," Julie shouted.

LeeAnn wiggled around, luxuriating. "Oh my God. I want to stay here forever!"

They laughed and looked at each other, sharing a moment.

"This thing must've cost tons," LeeAnn said. She ran her fingers through the plush purple shag. "They upholstered it with sheep fur!"

Julie glanced at her. "What?"

"Sheep fur. You know…what's on sheep?" LeeAnn's expression turned into one that Julie knew too well: a vulnerable, uncertain look.

Any other time, Julie would have plunged the knife in to the handle, destroying LeeAnn with a cutting remark. But Julie was feeling too good. And besides, LeeAnn looked cute. Kind of yummy, sunk in the cushions with her red jumpsuit. "Right," Julie said. "Hey, we better take the water."

Back at the stand, a slick young man in sunglasses walked up. "Hi. Are you girls the ones who make out?"

LeeAnn folded her arms. She sneered. "No."

Damn, Julie thought.

"This is the water stand, right?" The guy removed his shades and looked around as if he owned the place. "I heard the water stand girls were kissing and stuff."

"You heard wrong."

The man grinned. "I think I heard right." He departed.

"God, can you believe that?" LeeAnn said to Julie.

"Yeah, no kidding," Julie said.

"'Are you the girls who make out.' Gag me!" LeeAnn shoved a finger down her throat and pretended to retch. "Like I would ever, ever do that again. No offense."

"None taken."

Julie's mind raced. She added: "But, what if…"

"What?"

"No, nothing."

LeeAnn's big blue eyes grew wide. "What? No, really. Tell me!"

"Well, I was just thinking."

"Yeah?"

"Now—me, personally, I'm sort of considering going out to Los Angeles. Trying out for some TV and movie work, you know?"

LeeAnn gasped. Her palm slapped her chest, making her big boobs wobble. "Me, too!"

Of course you are, Julie thought. Previously, the notion of LeeAnn copying her would have thrown Julie into a rage. But today was different.

"So," Julie went on, "a lot of these people here are *from* Los Angeles."

"Uh-huh?"

"So, when you—we—move out there, wouldn't it be nice if we had some contacts?"

LeeAnn's face looked blank.

Julie took a breath and tried to be patient. "What I'm saying is, if we can get some of these entertainment people to notice us, and maybe give us their card or something, when we move to Los Angeles we can call them and get something going easier than just knocking on doors, you know?"

A slow expression of understanding illuminated LeeAnn's pretty features. "And so, like, they will remember us!"

"Right!"

LeeAnn's face morphed into wariness. "Wait a minute. What if all they want us to do when we get there is make out, or something? I want to be taken seriously."

Julie struggled not to say the first thing that came to mind. "Look, LeeAnn. Let's just try to score some numbers. If we get 100 numbers, and 99 of them are bullshit, but one is the golden ticket that gets us the big break, or closer to it, then it's worth it, right?"

LeeAnn considered. "I guess so," she said finally. Then she looked wary again. "You keep saying 'us.'"

"Yeah?"

"No offense, but I want nothing to do with you after this concert's over."

Julie shrugged. "Rad. All we do is copy the contact information. You get one copy, I get the other."

LeeAnn thought about it a long time.

Please, please, please, Julie thought.

"Okay," LeeAnn finally said. "But the pact stands, forever. Nobody knows. Right?"

"Right!"

LeeAnn's eyes narrowed. "How come you're excited about this?"

Julie looked back in a so-cool way. "How come you're not?"

A ponytailed man who had stepped up to their stand took a step back, slightly startled, as LeeAnn turned to him and said: "Hi! Want to see us make out?"

Wow, Julie thought.

By the end of the day, Julie's lips were raw.

"Sorry," LeeAnn said. She inserted a fingernail into her mouth. "I forgot to take my gum out that last time."

"Yeah, I noticed," Julie said. *I still felt The Feeling, though,* she thought.

The hour was late. Time for the last song of

the evening. On the other side of the big curtain, Corey Hart was singing "Dark Sunglasses" while dressed appropriately.

"Are you going to the Bangles party?" LeeAnn asked. The Bangles had stopped by earlier. After receiving some water, and watching Julie and LeeAnn kiss on request, the band had invited them to a late-night party at a club in the city.

"Nah," Julie said. She yawned. "I'm tired."

"Me too. All this Frenching is exhausting."

I could keep doing it with you till sunrise, Julie thought. She felt a now-familiar tingle erupt through her skin at the notion of French-kissing LeeAnn some more…

"So what do you think?" LeeAnn asked.

Julie started. She realized LeeAnn had been asking her something. "What? Sorry."

LeeAnn frowned. "I said, so who should take these? You or me?"

She pointed. A pile of business cards and bits of paper with hastily scribbled phone numbers and names lay in an empty water carton under the stand.

"I don't care," Julie said.

"If you're going home, why don't you take them." LeeAnn nodded. "I think I'll check out the Bangles party. But I don't want to leave the cards here. I'd hate to lose all that hard work, ha!"

Two hours later Julie was in her bed, staring up at the ceiling. She'd come home, had a bite, stripped down to her underwear and gone to bed as usual. But fatigued as she was, her mind was still in no mood to shut down.

How could this happen?

She shivered in the dark room. LeeAnn was the absolute last person on earth that Julie would ever have thought she'd be attracted to. The girl was stupid. Her boobs were too big. She had a loud laugh. LeeAnn was SO ANNOYING.

But let's face it, Julie thought. She sighed and closed her eyes.

LeeAnn turns you on.

There it was. Julie could argue with it, deny it, write a book about how such a thing was totally impossible. But she knew deep down what the facts were.

Okay, Julie told herself. She took a breath.

You are a rational person. And rational people made rational decisions.

So, fact number 1: LeeAnn turns you on.

There really wasn't any fact number 2.

Fine. Then the question is…what are you going to do about it?

Well, that seemed pretty obvious. Either Julie was going to seduce LeeAnn, or not.

Julie giggled. She covered her hands with her face. It was late, she was exhausted, and she always got silly when she felt super tired. But the idea. The IDEA of seducing LeeAnn Travis! It was far and away the silliest thing she had ever thought.

Except that when her mind created an image

of her and LeeAnn in bed, naked…Julie's heart hammered even harder than it had during their make-out sessions that day. Julie had not thought it could even be possible.

When finally her pulse had slowed, Julie tried to return to a rational approach.

Sex with a girl.

Hmm.

When she had been younger, Julie sometimes would sneak a look at porno magazines. Her dad had a secret stash. Didn't everybody's?

Occasionally the magazine would contain pictures of girls together. The photos had done nothing for Julie. They had not interested her at all.

After today's revelation of how LeeAnn gave Julie The Feeling, however, Julie was extremely interested in having her and LeeAnn re-creating some of those photos. Having LeeAnn all to herself, undressing her, doing whatever she wanted with LeeAnn's naked body—

THUMP THUMP THUMP. Julie heard her heart banging in her ears, a kettle drum.

She sighed.

There was just one small problem.

Julie and LeeAnn's hottest make-out that day had had Jani Lane of Warrant as an amused member of the crowd. He had been wandering nearby, guzzling a bottle of Wild Turkey, and had come over to see what all the commotion was about. LeeAnn had noticed him and had gone the extra mile. She had crushed Julie into her arms, kissing her deep. Julie had moaned. It had felt SO GOOD.

But when it was over and the Warrant frontman had departed with everybody else, LeeAnn had simply checked her make-up with her compact mirror.

Julie could tell that LeeAnn was not feeling it.

Julie rolled her head over her pillow and massaged her temples. Sometimes this exercise helped her to think. *Okay,* she considered. *LeeAnn is not feeling what you are feeling. Either that's going to stay the same, or it's going to change.*

She paused. *Can I help make it change?*

Julie remembered a particular date she'd had with a boy named Ronaldo. He had brought her home late. She had not invited him in. So he had kissed her good night. But the sneaky Ronaldo had turned one goodbye kiss into…well. Suffice to say, Julie had finally asked him inside.

What did he do? Something with my ears, and neck…

As the minutes passed, Julie's head turned and she closed her eyes, thinking of LeeAnn. Her hands slowly slid down over her belly button and into her panties.

* * *

Julie tapped the water bottle stand's plywood counter with an impatient finger. She had arrived early. Since she couldn't sleep, she had figured: *Why not?*

After much thought, Julie had dressed in a

white spaghetti-strap top with tiny stretch-ribs running up and down the thin fabric. It was actually a man's muscle shirt, something her ex-boyfriend (from whom she had stolen it) had called a wifebeater. It hugged Julie's boobs and flat stomach tight. The white cotton contrasted nicely with her creamy mocha skin. *Ah, the benefits of being half-Cuban!*

Julie glanced down. Her acid-washed jeans were perfectly ripped here and there. She hadn't ripped them herself. She had bought the jeans in a boutique, pre-ripped. They had cost a staggering piece of change. But they exposed exactly enough skin to make a boy (and, who knew, maybe LeeAnn) look twice, but didn't show enough to provoke some stupid woman professor at Daytona Community College into asking Julie to leave her class. Julie had friends that that had happened to.

Julie brightened. *There she is!*

LeeAnn yawned as she walked down the busy corridor toward the bottled water stand. The backstage pass on the lanyard around her neck slid back and forth over her big boobs. Her natural walk was part sashay. She had tied her hair into a kind of big side-pigtail, and she wore a leotard just like the girl in the new movie *Flashdance*, except that LeeAnn's was cheetah print. A multi-hued ruffle chiffon skirt and knee-high black buckle boots completed her ensemble. Julie had to admit, when it came to sexy, LeeAnn had a PhD.

"Hey," LeeAnn mumbled as she joined Julie behind the stand.

"Hey!"

LeeAnn eyed Julie suspiciously. "What's up?"

"What do you mean?"

"How come you're so happy?"

"Nothing. I'm a happy person." Julie tried not to stare at LeeAnn's boobs.

"That's news." LeeAnn yawned again.

Julie ignored the dig. "How was the Bangles party?"

LeeAnn grew animated. "Bitchin'. Although they said Prince was going to show up, but he didn't."

"I don't think Prince is scheduled to perform at this festival."

"Yeah, that's what they said."

"Then…why would anybody think he was going to show up here, in Daytona, at a Bangles party?"

"Because," LeeAnn said in an offended tone, "they are friends."

Julie made an oooo-kay face.

"I know, right?" LeeAnn said, misunderstanding Julie's expression. "Like, it's totally bogus. Why wasn't Prince invited to the festival?"

"I don't know," Julie said, trying to follow the slow unspooling of LeeAnn's thoughts.

"You know who also should have been

invited?" the blonde asked.

"Who?" *Here it comes,* Julie thought. *Some doofus Tony Orlando bullshit or something.*

"These guys." From some hidden pocket LeeAnn pulled out a cassette tape. She held it up for LeeAnn to see. There was no label but on the plastic were scratched the words: *Dead Milkmen.*

"Oh my gosh," Julie gasped. She looked at LeeAnn with wonder. "You know the Dead Milkmen?"

LeeAnn's eyes grew wide. "You do too?"

"Duh!"

"No duh!"

They jumped and squealed.

"Daytona CC radio played them once," Julie said. "God, they played a song, 'Bitchin' Camaro…'"

"It's on here!"

"No way."

"Way."

"How did you get that tape?"

LeeAnn shrugged modestly. "I know a guy. He lives in Philly. He sends me tapes. Here." LeeAnn offered the cassette. "You can borrow it."

"Mean it?"

"For certain. I'll still see you tomorrow, right?"

"For certain. I'll give it back then." Julie accepted the tape. She looked at it like it was a thousand-dollar bill.

LeeAnn grinned. "There's a song on there called Sri Lanka Sex Hotel. The guy in Philly says this is the only tape in the world that has that song."

Then how could he dub it onto this tape? Julie wondered. She decided not to ask. "Thanks LeeAnn."

"Sure."

The girls traded their first sincere smile in the history of their relationship.

LeeAnn's head swiveled. "Dude!"

A teenager paused as he hurried by. He carried a flat of convenience-store coffees in Styrofoam cups, precariously balanced above another flat of bagels.

"Come over here," LeeAnn said.

He did.

"How about a coffee and a bagel for me and my partner?" LeeAnn asked.

The teenager grinned. "Make out, and you got it."

Julie turned to LeeAnn—

But LeeAnn ignored her. "Ugh," LeeAnn groaned. "Kid, it's early. Just give us the freakin' coffee and bagel, or we will find your mother and tell her you are a delinquent."

The boy finally gave them two hot coffees, creamer (neither of the girls used saccharine), bagels, a plastic knife, and cream cheese in little toothpaste tubes.

"Awesome," Julie said through her chewing after the kid had left for the VIP lounge.

LeeAnn shrugged. "Now I have coffee breath.

Nice for when we make out. Woohoo. Speaking of which, I smoked two cigarettes on the way here. Sorry."

"I don't care," Julie said. She meant it.

Hours and many make-outs later, the bottles of water under the stand had disappeared.

Finally, Julie thought. Now, at last, she would be able to try out her plan. But first, she had to wait for LeeAnn to finish talking about her latest theory.

The morning had gone swimmingly. LeeAnn had been more relaxed while kissing than she had been the day before. She had even giggled a little. Agents, managers, and promoters (male and female) had all offered their business cards. The consensus among the important-looking people seemed to be that Julie and LeeAnn possessed serious potential as music-video vixens.

Part of Julie's strategy with LeeAnn had been to let LeeAnn talk about whatever she wanted. Then Julie would act interested. Julie had been played that way plenty of times on first dates.

So far, it seemed to be working. After starting cautiously, LeeAnn had opened up about all kinds of theories. She could talk about her theories all day long.

"So," LeeAnn said, "like, there's all this stuff about 'Shock The Monkey.' You know? Some people think the song's about animal rights. Other people think it's about some bizarre experiment with monkeys or whatever."

"Uh-huh." *How do boys do it?* Julie wondered. *Oh my gosh. If I have to listen to much more, I'll be running into traffic.*

"But my idea is THIS." LeeAnn smirked. "Peter Gabriel is talking about his dick."

"What?"

"The whole song. It's about his dick." LeeAnn raised her voice. John Cougar was ripping it up on stage and the crowd outside was going nutso. LeeAnn continued: "Like, you know, guys talk about spanking the monkey? Have you ever heard that?"

"Yeah…"

"Okay, so, shock the monkey. He wants to shock his monkey. Monn-keeee… Then he says, like, don't you monkey with the monkey. Basically he's saying that he jerks off a lot and it's not helping him. It's sort of a public service announcement."

"LeeAnn, that is…totally…one hundred and ten…the smartest thing I have ever heard, ever."

LeeAnn looked blushed. "You're the only person who thinks so. The only person who gets it, anyway."

"Coolness. Hey. We are out of water."

LeeAnn looked. "Oh. Yeah."

"Why don't we go get some more?"

In the stockroom, Julie hopped onto the purple couch. She patted the upholstery next to her. Giggling, LeeAnn leapt into the air and landed adjacent.

"This feels soooo good," Julie said. She rubbed her body against the plush like a cat.

"Yes," LeeAnn sighed. "I'd like to stay here forever."

Julie casually let her hand touch LeeAnn's. LeeAnn did not pull away. Their heads rested on the couch's back, staring at the ceiling.

"I'm really glad I got to do this with you," Julie said.

LeeAnn turned. Her blue eyes stared into Julie's. "Me too. You're not half the dork I thought you were."

"Loser!" Julie attacked. She managed to wrestle LeeAnn down onto the couch, pinning her.

"Geez, you're strong," LeeAnn said, laughing. She tried to push Julie off.

"I thought you'd have bigger muscles," Julie said. She nodded at the blonde's chest. "After all, you're carrying around those things all day."

LeeAnn's mouth made an O of outrage. She squealed, freed her hands and tickled Julie.

"Stop!" Julie shrieked and fell back. LeeAnn went on the offensive. She turned the tables on her adversary, straddling Julie on the big couch and holding her wrists down.

"Ooff. I surrender," Julie said. Their faces were inches apart.

"Say you're sorry," LeeAnn said. A weird light gleamed in her eyes. "Say it!"

"Okay. You're sorry."

LeeAnn doubled her tickling.

"Stop!" Julie screamed. She started to cry while laughing. "I'm sorry!"

LeeAnn paused. "Are you okay?"

"Yeah." Julie wiped a tear away. "I'm just super ticklish."

LeeAnn sat up again. Julie rose with her, adjusting her top. The wrestling session had displaced it. Then she glanced at LeeAnn: "Hold still."

Reaching with her finger, Julie carefully wiped away a smudge of lipstick near LeeAnn's mouth.

The blonde regarded her with a mix of shyness and suspicion. "Thank you."

"You're welcome." Julie wiped the lipstick on the inside of her shirt. "Hey. I had an idea."

"Okay."

"I think we should have a special kind of make-out that we can use. Something good. In case a big movie director comes by, or something."

LeeAnn shrugged. "I thought it was pretty good already. Nobody's complaining."

"Yeah, but. You know what I mean."

The blonde considered. "So what are you thinking?"

This is it, Julie thought. Casually, she said: "A nice, slow, sexy one. A good build-up."

LeeAnn frowned. "It sounds like it'll take a lot of time. What if people want water?"

Wow, Julie thought. "We can just put some

water on the counter. That way, if somebody's in a hurry, they could just take it and go."

"I don't know…"

"Yeah, me neither," Julie lied. "That's why we should try it out first."

"How?"

"Right here." Julie gestured at the room. "We can test."

LeeAnn still looked suspicious.

"Forget it," Julie said.

"No, I wasn't saying—"

"No really—"

"No, I get it," LeeAnn interrupted. "Let's do it."

In short order, Julie arranged LeeAnn and herself on the couch. They leaned with their sides against the backrest, facing each other. Their knees touched.

"Okay," Julie said. She ran her fingers over LeeAnn's ear, pushing soft blond hair behind it. "The trick is, we don't kiss."

"We don't?"

"Not right away." Julie touched LeeAnn's hand. "We build up to it."

LeeAnn's nose wrinkled as she squinted, trying to process.

"It's like, kind of, foreplay," Julie said.

A slow look of understanding passed over LeeAnn's features.

Julie smiled. "So, whoever's watching will be like, arrrg, just kiss already—"

"And we will hold back!" LeeAnn smiled and nodded, excited. "I know all about that."

Not from what I've heard, Julie thought to herself. "Okay," Julie said. "Just relax. You don't have to do anything."

Smiling, Julie moved her face forward until her lips brushed LeeAnn's ear.

"Ooh," LeeAnn said. She giggled and shivered. "Tingles."

Julie smiled bigger; LeeAnn couldn't see. With the lightest of touches, Julie ran her lower lip up and down the curve of LeeAnn's ear.

"Aah. God," LeeAnn said. She shivered again. "This might be too much. I'm kind of, like, sensitive."

Excellent. "Just relax," Julie ordered. "I'll try not to tickle you." It was true. Julie knew that if LeeAnn got too squirmy, she'd call the whole deal off.

Julie moistened her lips with her tongue. She left a slow trail of cool tiny kisses down LeeAnn's neck, from her ear curving down to below her Adam's apple.

"Whoa," LeeAnn murmured. Her tone was low and throaty.

Julie shifted slightly on the couch. Her boobs brushed LeeAnn's. Julie felt the blonde's lace bra under her shirt slide over her own. LeeAnn's nipples had hardened into headlights. *To think I was worried it might take forever to get her motor running,* Julie thought.

Indeed, the opposite problem happened. LeeAnn pulled back. She raised a hand. "Time out."

"What?" Julie asked. She wore her most innocent expression.

LeeAnn looked flushed and uncomfortable. "Like, so…"

Julie waited.

"It's kind of…"

Julie waited more.

Finally, LeeAnn spoke again. "It's kind of turning me on."

"Isn't that the whole point?"

"Huh?"

"You know about method acting, right?"

"No duh."

"And you want to act. That's what all this is about, right? Hollywood?"

"Sure."

"So," Julie said in her most reasonable voice, "if the point is to be exciting, and the performance is for us to look excited, that means actually feeling excited." Julie went on for another minute, talking about Stanislavski.

"I dunno," LeeAnn said.

"Well, never mind," Julie responded. She figured her forget-it strategy had worked earlier. Then she thought of something else. LeeAnn was competitive. She always had been. That was part of why she hated Julie so much. Julie was the only other girl in Daytona, or Florida for that matter, who could challenge her for the title of Hottest Girl.

"I'm not sure you can do it, anyway," Julie added.

"Say what?"

Julie made a kindly face. "Like, don't take this the wrong way, but it's just hard."

LeeAnn's eyes narrowed menacingly. "Are you saying I can't do it?"

"Look, it's cool." Julie stood up. "Why don't we get that water?"

Julie picked up a crate of water and walked to the door before LeeAnn could object. *Next time it will be ON,* Julie thought.

Back at the water stand, Marv was waiting.

"Uh-oh," the girls said in unison.

Sarcastically, Marv gestured to please return to their station behind the counter. Then he told Julie and LeeAnn that they were in big trouble.

"Or rather, you would be, under other circumstances," he said. "I've been waiting here over half an hour, wondering where you two were."

"Half an hour?" LeeAnn said.

Time really flew, Julie thought.

"Moreover, I understand that you two have been engaging in, shall we say, beyond-the-call-of-duty activities. Look. If you want to have some fun, fine. But you are rapidly becoming a distraction. So far, I've been ignorant. That's because I've been out. There are a bunch of stages at this festival. However, for the rest of today and tomorrow, consider yourselves under surveillance."

"We were just having fun…sir," Julie said.

"Really? I heard you were asking people if they were from L.A. It sounded like you were looking for contacts," Marv said. He eyed a few business cards that had been left on the stand counter while the girls had been away.

"Sorry," LeeAnn said.

"Under normal circumstances, if the rock stars are happy, I'm happy. But there comes a point when the stars can be *too* happy. When they start showing up to the stage late because they are hanging out here, for example, that's when we have a problem." Marv smiled a non-smile. "Bottom line: you are not fired. But you will be if you guys kiss even one more time. Clear?"

"Crystal," Julie said.

Marv considered them. "I'm probably digging my own grave. I have a feeling you girls shall be far more successful in the entertainment industry than I ever will be. So please, remember me charitably after you ascend Olympus. Meanwhile: no make-outs." He raised a finger in warning as he backed away. Then he was gone.

"Great," Julie said. She sighed. She dumped the business cards and numbers left on the counter into a box containing that day's contact offerings.

For the next few hours, Julie and LeeAnn did

not speak much. LeeAnn stared at the floor.

Finally, Julie asked: "Are you okay? Don't worry about that guy."

"I don't think I'm going to Los Angeles," LeeAnn said in a small voice.

"Huh? Why?"

Slowly, LeeAnn revealed her biggest insecurity: she thought Julie was prettier than she was.

"That's ridiculous," Julie said.

"No it's not," LeeAnn said. She sighed. "I'm…hot. Like, I have the body."

"Yes, you do," Julie said without thinking.

Something in Julie's voice made LeeAnn turn to her.

"But," LeeAnn finally continued, "your face is way, way more beautiful than mine. You model, for God's sake."

Julie made a weak attempt to dismiss it. But it was no use. It was true. Julie had done quite a bit of print work.

"I saw you in the Sears catalog," LeeAnn said.

"You did?"

"I've seen everything you've done." LeeAnn sighed. "I guess I could model bikinis for busty girls, or something. But I don't think my face is ever going to make me any money."

Julie argued. She told LeeAnn that she really was beautiful.

LeeAnn looked at her. Julie had never seen her so vulnerable. "You really mean it?" LeeAnn asked.

Impulsively, Julie leaned over and gave LeeAnn a quick smack on the lips.

Julie waited for LeeAnn to laugh. But the blonde only looked down. After a moment she said, "Thank you."

Under the counter, Julie reached and held LeeAnn's hand. LeeAnn squeezed it.

After another hour of handing out water, Julie and LeeAnn witnessed a sudden exodus. Streams of people flowed out the exits.

Julie grabbed a passing roadie. "What's going on?"

"MTV showed up," he said. "They're shooting live on the beach!"

In minutes, Julie and LeeAnn were manning a water booth in a completely deserted backstage.

Julie turned. "Want to go?"

LeeAnn shook her head.

"What's wrong?"

LeeAnn did not make eye contact. "I would've liked to have practiced some more."

After a moment, Julie said: "Well, we still can."

LeeAnn looked up. "Yeah?"

"Yeah. Sure. I mean, what if we go to an after party…"

"An after party," LeeAnn interrupted. "Yeah!"

"Like, we should have some skills."

"We totally need skills."

They smiled at each other.

Julie glanced at cartons of full bottles under the counter. "I suppose we could use some more water, too."

LeeAnn took Julie's hand and giggled. They hurried down the hall.

In the stockroom, Julie had barely switched the light on when LeeAnn flopped on the couch. She looked at Julie and crooked her finger: *c'mere*. Julie shut the door and locked it.

The moment Julie sat down, LeeAnn was kissing her.

"Um. Excuse me. Excuse me?" Julie said in a teasing way. She allowed LeeAnn to wrap her arms around and crush her into her body.

Julie murmured: "Practice. Remember?"

LeeAnn pulled away. She bit her lip. "Right."

Julie moved her face next to LeeAnn's, sliding cheek to cheek. She kissed LeeAnn's ear.

"You KNOW I'm sensitive there," LeeAnn said in a shaky voice.

Pulling back her lips, Julie nibbled the earlobe under the soft blonde hair.

"God, girl," LeeAnn whispered.

Julie brought a hand up to caress LeeAnn's other ear. As she did, her elbow brushed LeeAnn's breast. After a pause, Julie brushed it again, then again, slowly, back and forth, feeling LeeAnn's nipple harden under her stretchy cheetah-print fabric.

Not to be outdone, LeeAnn slipped her hand up to cup Julie's breast. Julie gasped.

"Two can play that game," LeeAnn whispered.

So competitive, Julie thought.

They made out. The energy was different from before. A current of hunger passed through their lips.

Suddenly the stockroom door handle rattled, making the locked door vibrate.

Startled, the girls pulled apart. Julie jumped up from the couch. LeeAnn followed.

A key turned in the lock. Marv burst in. "What the hell is going on!" He looked around as if expecting to find a wild party happening. "Nobody's at the water stand."

"We came to get some more water," Julie said.

Marv eyed her. "There's plenty of water there already."

"We just thought we'd get more," LeeAnn said.

"Since there wasn't many people around," Julie said. "You know. Get ready for the rush, when they'll all come back from the MTV shoot on the beach."

"Bullshit." Marv folded his arms. "Fool me twice. Give me your backstage passes, now. You two are officially fired."

* * *

Julie sat in her pajamas. She stared at the lime-green telephone on her kitchen wall. Then she looked at the table in front of her.

It was covered in business cards and slips of paper with telephone numbers. To one side were sheets of paper with all the cards and phone numbers carefully photocopied.

When Marv had fired them, Julie had insisted on returning to the stand to retrieve her purse. She had scooped up that day's pile of contacts while she was there. But when she returned to the stockroom, LeeAnn was gone. Marv had instructed security to escort her out.

After copying all the contact information, Julie had waited two days. She had hoped against hope that LeeAnn would call her or drop by. True, LeeAnn did not know where she lived, but Julie was listed in the phone book, just like LeeAnn.

Julie sighed. The rock festival was over. It was Saturday night. LeeAnn would almost certainly be out with friends. But somehow that made it easier for Julie to call, knowing that LeeAnn probably wouldn't be there.

Julie looked up LeeAnn's number in the phone book. It wasn't necessary. She now knew it by heart; she had been staring at it for the past two days.

After one ring, someone picked up.

"Hello?" LeeAnn asked.

"Oh, uh, hey," Julie stuttered. She had rehearsed a speech to give to LeeAnn's parents, figuring that they would take a message. But Julie had not prepared to speak to LeeAnn.

"Hey." LeeAnn's voice was filled with wonder.

"How's it going?" Julie asked after a pause.

"Fine. Did you get your purse?"

"Yeah. Um. Sorry I didn't say goodbye or anything."

"Don't apologize."

"It was just like, I went back, but you were gone—"

"Yeah, I know. I wanted to wait. But some gigantic security guy said that if I didn't have a backstage pass I had to go. He kind of dragged me out."

"Oh," Julie said.

"I almost called you."

Julie's heart skipped a beat. "Really?"

"Yeah. In fact, I was about to, this minute." LeeAnn laughed. "And then I was reaching for the phone and…it rang and scared me, and then it was your voice, and it was all kind of weird."

"Twilight Zone."

"Totally."

A long pause followed.

"Um, so," Julie said. "I was wondering if you wanted to come over or something."

Silence.

"It's just that I copied all those cards and stuff," Julie added in a rush, "and—"

"I want to come over," LeeAnn said.

"Oh. Okay. Great! Yeah, well, I've got all the contacts copied, and I can give you back your Dead Milkmen tape."

"I don't care about the contacts. Or the tape."

"Oh."

LeeAnn confirmed that Julie lived at the address listed for her in the phone book.

"So I guess I'll see you," Julie said.

"Yeah."

"Bye."

"Bye."

Julie hung up.

So she's coming over here, but she doesn't want the stuff, Julie thought. The notion filled her with anxiety.

What does she want then? Julie felt lightheaded.

Maybe she'll be like, Listen, it was fun, but we can't ever—

Julie heard a knock at the door.

Startled, she glanced at her watch. Twenty minutes had flown by. *Oh, great.* Julie looked down. She was still wearing her pajamas.

Opening the door, Julie greeted LeeAnn. The blonde was wearing bright stretchy pants and a tight T-shirt: *World Rock City, Daytona.*

"Nice," Julie said, nodding at the shirt.

LeeAnn looked down. She laughed. "I just grabbed the first thing in my drawer."

"Please don't tell me you got that for free. I totally forgot to get one."

"Okay, I won't tell you."

The girls smiled at each other.

"Um," LeeAnn said.

"Sorry. Come in."

Julie stepped aside and LeeAnn walked over the threshold. Julie closed the door and escorted her guest into the kitchen. They sat across from each other at the table.

"Nice place," LeeAnn said. She glanced at her

Dead Milkmen cassette, lying next to the copied contacts, but left it lying there.

"Thanks," Julie replied. "It's all right. It's a small house."

"You live alone?"

"Yeah."

LeeAnn nodded. "I live with my parents. Right, I think I told you that before."

"That's cool. No rent."

The blonde rolled her eyes. "Living with your parents blows."

"Yeah. Sorry."

Julie could feel it: her visceral attraction to LeeAnn. Every impulse in her body wanted to grab LeeAnn, kiss her, rip her clothes off.

But they only made small talk.

Finally, after more than an hour, LeeAnn sighed. "Well, I should go."

"Go?"

"I guess."

"Okay…if you want."

LeeAnn looked frustrated.

"What's up?" Julie asked.

LeeAnn closed her eyes. "Okay, I'm just going to say it. But just please tell me, no matter what happens, you won't spread it around about how, like, I am such a pathetic loser."

"No. I mean, no, you're not a loser. But yes, okay, whatever you want."

"I haven't slept the past couple of nights." LeeAnn stared at the floor. "All I can think about is kissing you."

Silence.

Julie's hand inched over the table toward LeeAnn's.

LeeAnn's hand moved, meeting Julie's.

"That's all I've been thinking about too," Julie said.

LeeAnn looked straight at Julie for the first time. *Her eyes are so blue,* Julie thought.

"Why don't we just do this," LeeAnn said. "We can figure it all out later."

"Okay," Julie said.

LeeAnn stood. Julie followed. LeeAnn walked out of the kitchen, looked around, turned, and led Julie by the hand down the hall toward the bedroom, as if LeeAnn were the one who lived there.

The bedroom was a disaster area. Dirty clothes covered the carpet. A few bowls and plates were stacked on the bedside table.

But LeeAnn stared only at a page of a magazine that had been carefully cut and taped to the wall. It showed a close-up of Julie's smiling face for a makeup ad.

A turntable's needle scratched. LeeAnn looked over her shoulder.

Julie stood above a spinning record player. Smiling, she held up an album: *Synchronicity.* The beginning strains of "Every Breath You Take" began to play.

LeeAnn grinned. "You trying to say

something?"

Julie took a step toward her. "What would that be?"

"I dunno. Maybe that I've been watching you?"

Julie's hands touched LeeAnn's neck. "Have you?"

"I told you. I've seen everything you've done. That one's my favorite, by the way." LeeAnn thumbed over her shoulder at the magazine page.

"And why would that be?" Julie kissed LeeAnn's ear very softly.

"Because," LeeAnn said, trying not to gasp, "it shows off your pretty face."

LeeAnn placed her hands upon Julie's shoulders, taking control. She kissed her hard.

"Whoa," Julie said when she finally came up for air. She looked dizzy.

"I don't mean to be forward," LeeAnn murmured. She raised Julie's arms and gently pulled her pajama top up and off.

"Uh, okay…" Julie was wearing no bra. She tried to act cool, but she could barely think. *This is happening,* she thought. *This is really happening.*

LeeAnn grinned. She pulled her own shirt off with a quick easy movement.

"Wow," Julie said.

The blonde blinked. "What?"

Julie stared at LeeAnn's chest. Her big boobs strained the fabric of her plain white bra. "You really are the hottest girl in Daytona."

LeeAnn laughed. She reached, took Julie's hand, and placed it upon her breast.

Julie felt the soft foam cup of the bra and wondered why nothing like this had ever turned her on so much before.

"You can take it off," LeeAnn whispered. She tilted her face slightly and began kissing Julie's mouth with slow, sexy lips.

Focus, Julie thought. But it was hard to think. LeeAnn had short-circuited her brain.

LeeAnn snaked her arms around Julie, crushing her hard. A hunger radiated from LeeAnn. She began slipping her hands down inside Julie's pajama bottoms, massaging her ass. Julie realized that the blonde was not going to stop even if Julie wanted her to.

Julie fiddled with LeeAnn's bra snap and finally managed to undo it.

LeeAnn pulled away for just long enough to flip the wall switch. The room went dark.

"Hi," LeeAnn giggled in the pitch black. Julie's eyes tried to adjust. LeeAnn's eyes were quicker; her tongue snaked out and licked Julie's nipple, quick as a whip.

"Aaah," Julie said. She covered her chest.

"Aww, I'm sorry," LeeAnn purred. She pulled Julie by the shoulders over to the bed. "Mind if I make myself more comfortable?" Without waiting for an answer, LeeAnn leaped upon the mattress. The springs creaked.

What's gotten into her? Julie wondered. *Well, she*

never did lack for confidence. Julie's eyes had adjusted to the gloom. She crawled upon the bed, moving for LeeAnn, who had already unzipped and removed her jeans.

"Ah, there you are," LeeAnn breathed. She placed her hand behind Julie's head and kissed her deeply, pushing her tongue deep. Julie moaned.

"God, you sexy girl," LeeAnn whispered. She slipped her body under Julie's, raising her hands to massage her host's breasts.

Julie moaned. She twisted her body out of LeeAnn's grasp, moving down. LeeAnn used her elbows to scoot up, helping. Her head and shoulders rested on a pile of pillows against the headboard.

Julie bit her lip. LeeAnn's panties were plain white cotton. Even in the dark, Julie could see a long wet spot in the middle of the crotch. LeeAnn lifted her knees and ankles, and waited.

After a long moment, Julie slid the panties up and off of LeeAnn. As an afterthought, she removed LeeAnn's ankle socks, also.

"What liberties you take," LeeAnn said. But a tremor in her voice betrayed her excitement.

LeeAnn Travis is naked in my bed, thought Julie. She took a moment to give her one-time rival a good long look.

The hourglass blonde tilted her hip and smirked, posing for an appreciative audience. Her hair had spilled over the pillow. Her big breasts rose and lowered with her rapid breathing. Even the harshest critic would have to admit: LeeAnn looked outstanding.

"I want to take a picture," Julie said without thinking.

LeeAnn giggled. "I'll give you mine if you give me yours."

Julie kissed her knee. LeeAnn raised it up high, beckoning. Julie crawled under LeeAnn's leg, settling onto the bed between her thighs.

Moving her torso higher, Julie kissed LeeAnn's flat stomach just below her navel. The blonde gasped.

Lowering her shoulders again, the brunette stared. A thick triangle of golden curls gleamed with wetness, inches from Julie's face. She could smell LeeAnn's sweet strong scent.

Wow, Julie thought. Her mind shifted as she seemed to go to a different place.

Like a patient waking from hypnosis, Julie was brought back to reality by a gentle tug. LeeAnn's hands had encircled Julie's head. Her face was being pulled, closer and closer, to the blond thatch.

What happened? Julie thought. *Did I just…check out?* She wondered how long she had been frozen, staring at…

…LeeAnn's mons, now tilting up to kiss her.

Julie's eyes closed as her lips brushed the pubic hair. A few sharp wet curls slipped into her mouth. LeeAnn tasted exquisite.

Moving her lips slowly through the wet bush, Julie placed kiss after kiss all around LeeAnn's vulva.

"Oooohhhh," LeeAnn moaned.

After many circuits around the labia, Julie pressed her lips upon the warm wet slit. Opening her mouth, she began to explore LeeAnn with her tongue.

The blonde began rolling her hips up and down, up and down, as if performing a slow-motion bellydance.

Julie kept her mouth upon LeeAnn. Moaning, she wrapped her arms around the blonde's thighs, holding on as LeeAnn's bucking grew more violent.

"Oh God," LeeAnn said with an intensity Julie had never heard from a person before.

Suddenly, the blonde spasmed. Her fingernails scratched the sheets as she wailed a long, loud cry. Her convulsion knocked the bed against the wall; the record player skipped.

Julie looked up. LeeAnn's body was covered in slick cold sweat. She gulped big bites of air.

"Hi," Julie whispered. She giggled and kissed LeeAnn's thigh, nuzzling her cheek against wet blonde curls.

LeeAnn seemed barely alive.

Julie looked down. LeeAnn's damp bush beckoned to her. She giggled again, pushed her face into it, and gave it an extra-loud smack.

LeeAnn jumped. Moaning, she reached down

and clawed, seizing Julie's arm.

Julie allowed herself to be pulled up. She collapsed next to LeeAnn, grinning at her onetime adversary, who didn't seem to be able to catch her breath. Silky blonde hair was stuck to her wet face.

"Hi," Julie repeated. She hid part of her face behind a pillow playfully.

"Thunderballs," LeeAnn finally said.

Julie laughed. "I've never heard that one."

"I never said it before. I don't know where that came from."

"Interesting."

LeeAnn stared at Julie. Her eyes had never looked so blue. She wiped damp hair from her face. "Have you done that before?"

"Uh. That would be a no."

"B.S."

"Swear-true." Julie made a little hook with her pinky and lifted it up.

"Wow." LeeAnn inhaled another lungful of air and exhaled slowly. "I got the tingles all over." She raised her arms, examining them. "Look."

Indeed, tiny goosebump pimples covered LeeAnn's creamy skin.

Julie giggled again. She kissed the underside of LeeAnn's big breast, feeling the bumps harden like stubble under her tongue. LeeAnn gasped. She struggled with Julie as Julie tried to lick higher, toward the summit.

"Quit!" LeeAnn exclaimed. "You're going to

make me crazy."

Julie bit her lip, grinning. "So?"

LeeAnn had maneuvered into the superior position, holding Julie down. She seemed to be thinking hard.

"What's up?" Julie asked.

"Nothing. Nothing that I haven't already said, anyway. You're pretty."

Without waiting for a response, LeeAnn bent her head. She kissed and licked Julie's neck while holding her host's wrists down.

"Ha ha," Julie said in a nyah-nyah tone. "I'm not ticklish." It was a total lie. Julie only barely managed to keep herself under control as LeeAnn's lips brushed over her flawless olive skin.

"Hey," Julie added. "Kiss?" She felt if LeeAnn did not stop, she'd jump through the ceiling.

LeeAnn rose and made out with her. Julie was surprised, and touched, by the blonde's tenderness.

"I like you," LeeAnn whispered finally. "I mean it."

"I like you too," Julie said, hearing her voice catch.

They kissed a long time, letting a slow deep rich heat build, like a simmering dish that could be brought to boil at any moment.

At length, LeeAnn began to kiss her way down Julie's chest.

Julie ran her fingers gently through LeeAnn's

long blond locks, watching the beautiful girl move her naked body down inch by inch in the dark.

At length, LeeAnn kissed her way past Julie's navel. She stared at a small dark triangle of shiny hair between Julie's tightly-pressed legs.

Keeping her eyes on Julie's thatch, LeeAnn moved her body so that she was lying on her side at a right angle to her host. She lifted her face directly over the intersection of Julie's legs, hovering.

She hesitated. Her breathing grew labored.

Julie placed her hand on LeeAnn's butt, a gentle easy touch.

The blonde closed her eyes and lowered her lips into Julie's pubic hair. She placed a gentle kiss before lifting her head again.

"Oh," Julie said softly. She parted her knees just the tiniest bit.

LeeAnn rubbed her fingers through the dark curls, staring down expressionlessly. She lowered her face once more and kissed again, longer this time.

THUMP-THUMP-THUMP. Julie felt her heart about to explode, but this time she felt no fear. *I'll die happy,* she thought. Trying not to tremble, she parted her legs.

LeeAnn carefully moved her long blonde hair up and over her shoulders. She shifted her body, turning her stomach onto the mattress and sliding one arm around Julie's shaking thigh. "Yes,"

LeeAnn whispered. She closed her eyes and ran her tongue in circles within Julie's damp pubic hair, moving in an ever-closing spiral. When her tongue finally rested at the top of Julie's opening, the brunette cried out.

LeeAnn lowered her lips and began to taste Julie, sliding her mouth up and down with slow languorous movements.

"Wow," Julie herself say. Her hand found LeeAnn's; they interlocked fingers, holding tight, sharing the moment. "Oh. God. LeeAnn. You…"

The orgasm rose inside of Julie like a wave before crashing inside of her, flooding her body with ecstasy. "Oh," she gasped in a keening moan. "Oooohhhhh…"

After Julie had finally caught her breath, she opened her eyes to see LeeAnn's face over hers, smiling. "Did I do good?" LeeAnn whispered, giggling.

Julie felt too buzzed to reply. She reached up with shaky arms and pulled her lover down. They embraced.

Later they would discuss plans—going to Los Angeles, getting an apartment together, and whether or not they should share one car between them. But for now, they simply held each other on the bed in the dark room, listening to every breath the other took.

The End

Thanks for reading! If you have time, please review *Rock City*. I read every review, and I appreciate honest feedback!

If you enjoyed this book, you may also enjoy

The Beard

By Anne Eton

When tall, pretty Kelly interviews at Washington D.C.'s premier LGBT-centric lobbying firm, she claims she has a girlfriend. Nothing could be further from the truth; she's never even kissed a girl. Kelly's hired. However, a suspicious co-worker keeps inquiring about her girlfriend. To keep her lies straight, Kelly bases her fictional partner on Anna, an aggressive, gorgeous lesbian friend of a friend. But when the firm's annual Christmas party looms, Kelly's forced to produce her mysterious girlfriend. The real Anna agrees to be Kelly's "beard"—her fake date. But at the party, alcohol flows... and Anna's all over Kelly. Kelly pretends to her office mates that her "girlfriend's" advances are perfectly normal—even as she feels her resistance to the beautiful woman melting away.

The Beard is a comedy with sexy scenes and some explicit passages.

Excerpt follows!

The Beard

Excerpt:

Kelly stumbled, tipsy. Anna guided her with a sure hand to the office supply room, opening the door and escorting her inside.

"Hey! Office supplies," Kelly said with false cheer. She looked around nervously. "You need some gel pens? Ha, ha!"

Anna smirked. She shut the door behind them and pressed the doorknob's button, locking it.

"Or paper clips, or toner," Kelly babbled, casually backing away. "It's a regular Staples in here!"

"Yes," Anna replied. The blonde gave Anna a sexy look and flipped a wall switch. The room went dark.

"I think we should talk about expectations," Kelly said in the pitch black, as if discussing the price of a car. "I admit, I did sort of use you for my own ends…"

"Yes."

Kelly felt Anna's hands. The tall girl backed away; she came up against waist-high pallets of paper boxes.

"You see," Kelly gasped, "I know we're supposed to be pretending that you're my girlfriend—"

"Yes… yes…" Anna murmured. She began slipping Kelly's dress up as the taller girl moved awkwardly against the immovable cartons.

Also by Anne Eton

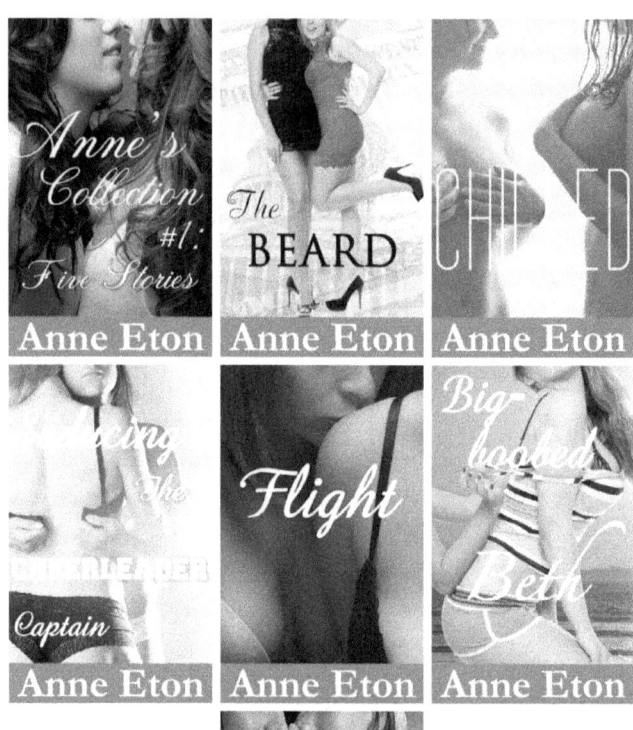

ABOUT THE AUTHOR

I write first-time F/F erotic romance. I love what I do!

If you would like to know when I publish new books, please join my New Release Mailing List, at my site! I don't share my readers' email with anyone, for any reason.

www.anneeton.com

Thanks for reading!

Anne